Making Frien Is an Art!

Written by **Julia Cook**

Illustrated by **Bridget A. Barnes**

To Joy – EGTBOK
          ~Love, Julia

Thank you Terri!

BOYS TOWN
Press

Boys Town, Nebraska

Making Friends Is an Art!
Text and Illustrations Copyright © 2012, by Father Flanagan's Boys' Home
ISBN 978-1-934490-30-3

Published by the Boys Town Press
14100 Crawford St.
Boys Town, NE 68010

Page Design: Anne Hughes

For a Boys Town Press catalog, call **1-800-282-6657**
or visit our website: **BoysTownPress.org**

Publisher's Cataloging-in-Publication Data

Cook, Julia, 1964-

Making friends is an art! / written by Julia Cook ; illustrated by Bridget A. Barnes. --
Boys Town, NE : Boys Town Press, c2012.

p. ; cm.
(Building relationships ; 1st)

ISBN: 978-1-934490-30-3

Audience: grades 3-8.
Summary: Meet Brown, the least used pencil in the box. He discovers that in order to have friends, he needs to be a good friend. If Brown learns to use all of the friendship skills the other pencils have, he can make friends and have fun, too.

1. Friendship--Juvenile fiction. 2. Interpersonal relations in children--Juvenile fiction.
3. Children--Life skills guides--Juvenile fiction. 4. [Friendship--Fiction. 5. Interpersonal relations--Fiction.] I. Barnes, Bridget A. II. Title. III. Series: Building relationships ; no. 1.

PZ7.C76984 M35 2012

E   1202

Printed in the United States
10 9 8 7 6 5 4 3

Boys Town Press is the publishing division of Boys Town, a national organization serving children and families.

My name is **Brown**.

I spend a lot of my time in a pencil box with a bunch of other colors.

We are all different. Some of us are sharper than others.
Some of us are long and others are short.

And then there's **Red**. Everybody loves **Red**.
She's been sharpened so much that now she's stubby.

We are all supposed to be friends,
but I don't feel like I fit in very well.

First of all, I'm **Brown** ... not exactly a favorite color.
I don't get to color a lot like some of the others.

I'm the tallest pencil in the box
because I rarely need
to get sharpened.

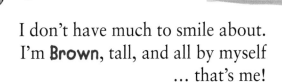

I don't have much to smile about.
I'm **Brown**, tall, and all by myself
... that's me!

5

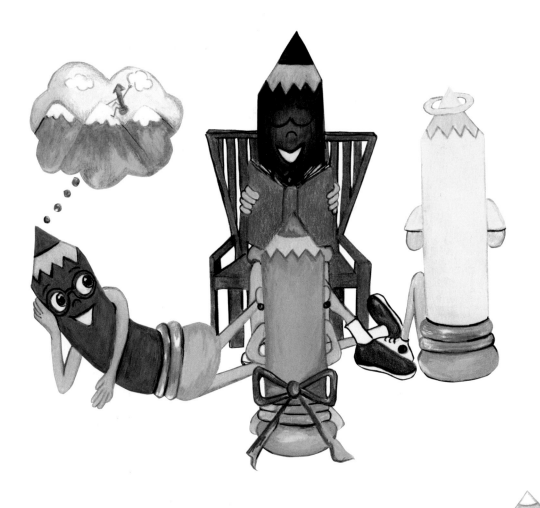

I wish I could be like the
other colors:

Black looks out for all of us.

Yellow always does what's right.

Purple has hopes and dreams, and

White won't let us fight.

Dark Green is very trustworthy.

Pink listens to everyone.

Light Green is always honest, and

Orange just likes to have fun.

Blue gives all of us hugs
whenever we feel down.
Red does things with everyone,
and then there's me ... just Brown.

Sometimes, I complain a lot
to the other colors around.
At times, I'm disrespectful
and I usually wear a frown.

I hardly ever laugh
but the others laugh at me.
It's hard to be kind to them
and show them empathy.

Yesterday, we were doing an art project at school,
and I was the only color in the box that didn't get used.
Red got used so much that she had to get sharpened again!

Everyone likes **Red**, but nobody likes me.

I wish I could be more like **Red**.

I went to talk to Blue. She gave me a big hug,
but all she said was, "Making friends is a true art, Brown.
You just need to figure out how to use the right colors."

I had no idea what **Blue** was talking about, so I went to find Light Green because I knew he would be honest with me.

"Friendship is one of the most precious gifts that there is," he said.
"But to have good friends, you need to be a good friend,
  and, **Brown**, you just aren't a very good friend.
  That's why the rest of us don't like to hang out with you."

"What's wrong with me?" I asked.

14

"**Brown**, you never laugh,
and you always put us down.
You think our opinions are silly,
and you usually wear a frown.

You like to disagree
with everything we say,
and you always complain,
like every single day!

You don't even try to understand
where we are coming from.
Brown, doing things with you
just isn't that much fun!"

"Wow! That's a lot of stuff!" I said.

"My point is, **Brown**, that in order to have good friends,
you need to be a good friend. Besides, having good friends
can make you a better person."

I thought about everything that Light Green said,
and then I went to talk to **Red**.

"You're so lucky, **Red**! You have so many friends
and you get to color more than anyone.
I wish I was like you!"

"Well," said **Red**. "I wish I was still tall like you!
Sometimes I get tired of coloring so much,
and getting sharpened gives me a headache.
Now, I'm so stubby that I can't even see
outside of the pencil box.

I would give anything to be tall again like you."

"As far as the friend thing goes,
even having just one good friend
can make a big difference.

But **Brown**, you have to know how to be
a good friend in order to make friends.

You can start by figuring out a way
to be your own best friend.

You can't expect the other colors
to like you if you don't like yourself."

"There's not much to like," I said.

"Well, I see lots to like:

You're tall.

You're sharp,

and you get to be **Brown**!

Lucky you!!"

"How is being **Brown** lucky?"

"**Brown** is a very special color.
Once you realize that,
you'll have more pencil friends
than you know what to do with.
And you just can't have too many friends!"

I went to talk to **Black**.

"**Red** says I'm special because I'm **Brown**."

"That you are," said **Black**.

"Why?" I asked.

"Haven't you noticed that when all of us are mixed together we make **Brown**?
You are a combination of all the colors. You just don't realize it yet,
but you have everything inside you that it takes to be a great friend."

"Your **Black** can look out for all of us.
Your Yellow can show us what's right.
Your **Purple** can give us all hopes and dreams,
and your White can help us not fight."

"Your **Dark Green** can be very trustworthy.
Your **Pink** can listen to everyone.
Your **Light Green** will always be honest,
and your **Orange** can help us have fun.

Your **Blue** can give us great hugs
whenever we're feeling down.
Your **Red** can do things with all of us.
See, you have it all, **Brown!**"

21

"Use all of the colors you're made of,
And learn to like yourself.
Develop a sense of humor.
It's good for pencil health.

Respect the rights of others.
Show empathy and be kind.
Be friendly and don't complain.
It will work for you every time."

I tried doing everything that **Black** told me to do, and guess what?

It really worked!

First of all, I made a promise to myself to stop putting other pencils down.

Since **Red** feels bad about being stubby, I figured out a way to help her.

I rolled around on a glue stick and glued her to my side so she could be tall again and see out of the pencil box!

I still don't get to color as much as
the other colors do, but that's okay.

Now I have more pencil friends
than I know what to do with!

But just like **Red** says,
you can't have too many friends.

I just LOVE being **Brown**!

"Class ... today I would like you to take out your colored pencils and draw a picture of a big **Brown** grizzly bear!"

Tips for Parents, Teachers, and Counselors

FRIENDSHIPS ARE VERY IMPORTANT when it comes to our emotional health! A lack of friends can have devastating effects on a child. Children who struggle with making and keeping friends often experience mental health problems such as anxiety and depression. They are also more likely to get into trouble and drop out of school.

To a child, having even just one good friend can make a huge difference. Research shows it is not the quantity of friends children have that matters, it's the quality of even one or two good relationships. You can help your children or students become better at making and keeping friends by teaching them three basic social skills:

- How to break the ice with kids they haven't met before.
- How to act positively with others.
- How to manage conflict constructively.

To teach these skills to a child, you must first figure out what the child is already doing right and then what the child needs to learn to do better. Specific needs vary from child to child and situation to situation. Here are some tips:

1 Observe your child objectively in social settings and compare his interactions to those of well-liked children.

2 Isolate the skill(s) that your child needs to learn or use more effectively. For example, does your child interrupt others, always try to "be the boss," act aggressively toward others, or cry and pout when things don't go his way? Or, is your child excessively shy and quiet around other children, afraid to try new activities, or reluctant to join a group?

3 Explain the steps of the skill to your child. Relate the skill to his world-view by attaching it to a situation the child has experienced. Demonstrate how to effectively use the skill. (For example: "You told me there's a new student in your class that you'd like to know and be friends with. If you want to introduce yourself to him, look at him, smile, and say something like 'Hi, my name is Jason. Would you like to play catch with me during recess?'")

4 Help your child practice the skill. ("Now pretend I'm the new student and introduce yourself to me. What would you say?")

5 Give your child constructive feedback. Always start by telling your child what he did right and then what he can improve on. Remember to teach … not criticize.

6 Be patient. Teaching social skills will never be as easy as it sounds, and we are all at different levels of learning. Always try to practice what you preach. Remember: Making friends is an ART! – so get out the pencils, practice, and use lots of paper!!!

For more parenting information, visit:

parenting.org™

from **BOYS TOWN.**

31

Boys Town Press Books by Julia Cook

Kid-friendly books to teach social skills

Reinforce the social skills RJ learns in each book by ordering its corresponding teacher's activity guide and skill posters.

 **Building** RELATIONSHIPS

A book series to help kids get along.

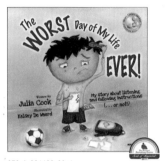

978-1-934490-20-4
978-1-934490-34-1 (Spanish)

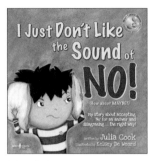

978-1-934490-25-9
978-1-934490-53-2 (Spanish)

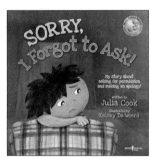

978-1-934490-28-0

978-1-934490-30-3

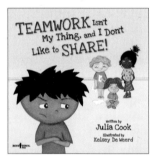

978-1-934490-35-8

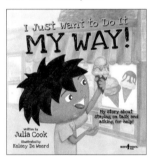

978-1-934490-43-3

978-1-934490-49-5

978-1-934490-39-6

978-1-934490-47-1

978-1-934490-23-5

978-1-934490-27-3

978-1-934490-32-7

978-1-934490-37-2

978-1-934490-45-7

978-1-934490-51-8

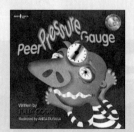

978-1-934490-48-8

Boys Town Education and Parenting Programs

For more information on Boys Town, its Education Model®, Common Sense Parenting®, and training programs, visit boystowntraining.org, or parenting.org, e-mail training@BoysTown.org, or call 1-800-545-5771.

For parenting and educational books and other resources, visit the Boys Town Press website at BoysTownPress.org, e-mail btpress@BoysTown.org, or call 1-800-282-6657.

 **BOYS TOWN®** Press

BoysTownPress.org